A PIG, A FOX, AND STINKY SOCKS

ISBN:
9780593432624

by Jonathan Fenske

Random House 🏠 New York

PART ONE

This pair of socks was on my feet.

This pair of socks does NOT smell sweet.

And hide inside
this handy pail.

To watch Pig find
his stinky mail.

12

PART TWO

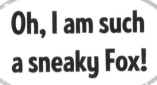

Another pair of socks that stink.
Another funny trick I think.

21

Here comes Pig! I must be quick!

This empty can should do the trick.

GARBAGE

But wait! What is inside my slop?

That sneaky Fox. He has to stop.

24

26

27

And so does Fox.

PART THREE

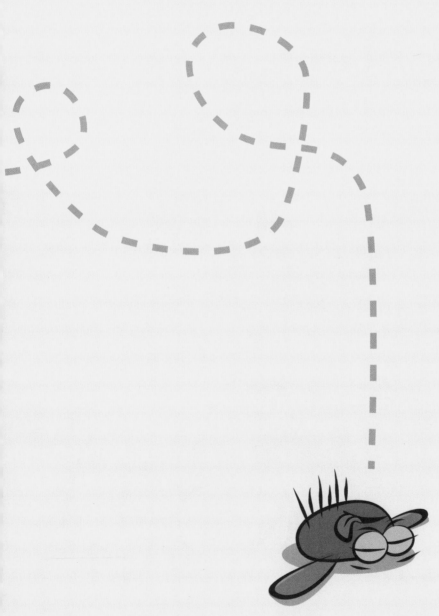